No More Vegetables!

NICOLE RUBEL

Farrar, Straus and Giroux

New York

For my niece, Rebecca, who didn't eat her vegetables

Copyright © 2002 by Nicole Rubel
All rights reserved
Distributed in Canada by Douglas & McIntyre Ltd.
Color separations by Prime Digital Media
Printed and bound in the United States of America by Berryville Graphics
First edition, 2002
1 3 5 7 9 10 8 6 4 2

Library of Congress Cataloging-in-Publication Data
Rubel, Nicole.
   No more vegetables! / Nicole Rubel.
      p. cm.
   Summary: When a young girl demands "No more vegetables," her mother
agrees as long as Ruthie helps in the vegetable garden.
   ISBN 0-374-36362-5
   [1. Vegetables—Fiction. 2. Gardening—Fiction. 3. Food
habits—Fiction.] I. Title.

PZ7.R828 Nm 2002
[E]—dc21
                                                                    2002020654

"NO MORE VEGETABLES!" said Ruthie at dinner one night.

She shared her peas and carrots with the dog.
"That's no way to join the clean-plate club," said Dad.
"Vegetables are gross!" said Ruthie.

"Why do I have to eat vegetables?" asked Ruthie.

"Because we love you and we want you to be healthy," said Mom.

"Potato chips and french fries are vegetables," said Ruthie as she enjoyed an after-school snack the next day. "Potato chips and french fries don't count," said her little brother.

That night Ruthie had a vegetable dream!

Mom took Ruthie to the doctor.

"Ruthie won't eat her vegetables," she said.

"Oh dear," said the doctor. "If you don't eat your vegetables, your ears will fall off and your skin will turn blue."

Ruthie caught him winking.

In school, Ruthie's teacher said, "The different food groups form a pyramid. I want each of you to tell me something about one of the food groups."

Food
Pyramid

Ruthie had something to say about vegetables.

Give me a yucky carrot,
I'll feed it to the parrot.

Offer me slimy beets,
I'll stomp them with my feets.

A heap of green peas
only makes me sneeze.

I was not born
to eat spinach and corn.

No more vegetables!

Ruthie said no thank you to zucchini muffins at
dinner that night.

"I give up," said Dad.

But Mom had an idea.

"Okay, Ruthie," she said. "No more vegetables for you.
IF you help me in my garden."

"Okay!" said Ruthie. "Growing vegetables must be better
than eating them."

Working in the garden wasn't bad at all.

Mom dug long rows in the ground while Ruthie dropped in seeds.

They planted carrots, tomatoes, string beans, and peas; cucumbers, red peppers, corn, and lettuce.

"Did you know that tomatoes are actually a fruit?" Mom asked.

Ruthie made a face. "I still don't like them."

One of Ruthie's jobs was to take care of the weeds that her mother missed.

"You don't belong here," she would scold as she yanked them out.

It was Ruthie who saved the garden from a slug invasion. "Keep away!" she warned the plant-eating pests.

At first, mealtime was a blast. Mom kept her word and no more vegetables landed on Ruthie's plate.
But after a while Ruthie began to feel something was missing.

One afternoon, Ruthie's dog spoiled her plans for a picnic. Ruthie was so hungry she popped a cherry tomato in her mouth. Not bad, she decided, and gobbled up some more.

Still starving, she picked a pea pod. The green peas nestled inside reminded her of candy. They tasted sweet, too.

Next, she chomped an ear of fresh corn. Delicious!

Then she nibbled a crunchy carrot. Outstanding!

Ruthie ate and ate.

Ruthie ate too much!

"What's wrong?" Mom asked.

Ruthie said, "No more vegetables . . .

. . . until dinnertime!"